The Berenstain Bears AND TOO MUCH JUNK FOOD

Healthy food is good
for Brother, Sis, and Dad...
How can Mom make them stop
eating food that is bad?

A FIRST TIME BOOK®

The Berenstain Bears
AND TOO MUCH

JUNK

Stan & Jan Berenstain

Random House New York

 Published in the United States by Random House, Inc., New York, and simultaneously in Canada by Random House of Canada Limited, Toronto.

Library of Congress Cataloging in Publication Data: Berenstain, Stan. The Berenstain bears and too much junk food. SUMMARY: Mama Bear starts a campaign to convince her family that they are eating too much junk food. 1. Children's stories, American. [1. Food, Junk—Fiction. 2. Food habits—Fiction. 3. Bears—Fiction] I. Berenstain, Jan. II. Title. PZ7.B4483Belp 1985 [E] 84-40393 ISBN: 0-394-87217-7 (trade); 0-394-97217-1 (lib. bdg.)

Manufactured in the United States of America

33 34 35 36 37 38 39 40

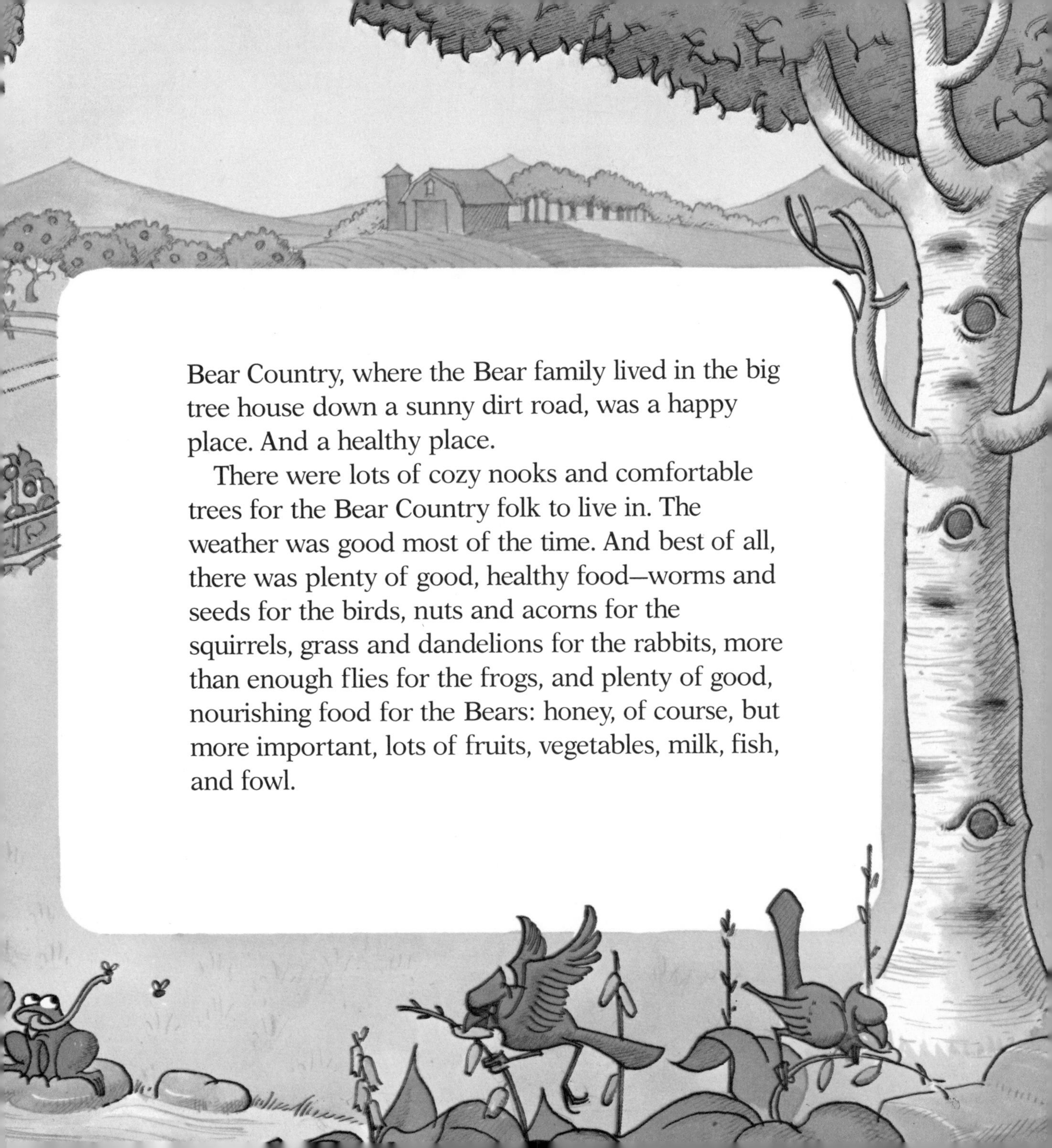

Bear Country, where the Bear family lived in the big tree house down a sunny dirt road, was a happy place. And a healthy place.

There were lots of cozy nooks and comfortable trees for the Bear Country folk to live in. The weather was good most of the time. And best of all, there was plenty of good, healthy food—worms and seeds for the birds, nuts and acorns for the squirrels, grass and dandelions for the rabbits, more than enough flies for the frogs, and plenty of good, nourishing food for the Bears: honey, of course, but more important, lots of fruits, vegetables, milk, fish, and fowl.

The trouble was that certain bears...

had gotten into the habit of
eating not-so-healthy foods...

when watching TV...

at the movies...

and at the mall.

In fact, it began to seem to Mama Bear that anytime was snack time.

At first she hadn't paid much attention, but then one day when the cubs were raiding the pantry, Mama noticed something. The cubs were getting a little chubby. She took a closer look just to be sure.

Yes, they were chubbier from the side...

they were chubbier from the front...

and from the back—

Well, there was no question about it. Brother and Sister were going to have to stop eating all that junk food!

"But, Mama!" they protested. "We're growing bears and we need those snacks!"

"You're growing, all right," said Mama. "The trouble is you're growing from side to side as much as you are up and down! Sometimes cubs get into bad habits, and you've gotten into the habit of eating altogether too many sweets and goodies...

"We're going to have to get back to healthy, nourishing food!" She gathered up all the goodies in one big load.

"Mama!" cried Sister Bear. "What are you doing?"

"You're not going to throw them away?" cried Brother.

"No, we're going to put them in the freezer and forget about them," she said. "And there's no use arguing!"

"That's right," agreed Papa, coming in from his shop. "There's no use arguing with your mother when she's made up her mind." Then, looking into the refrigerator, he said, "Oh, dear! We're out of Sweetsie-Cola. Let's be sure to get some next time we're at the supermarket."

"Our Sweetsie-Cola days are over," said Mama. As she pushed all the goodies into the freezer, two packages fell to the floor.

"Say!" shouted Papa. "What are you doing with my Sugar Balls and Choco-Chums?"

"They're going into the freezer and we're going to forget about them!" cried Brother. "We're going to eat healthy, nourishing food instead!"

"Just a minute!" said Papa. But as he leaned over to pick up his precious goodies, there was a loud r-r-r-i-p! Papa's snack habits had caught up with him, too. He had split the seat of his overalls wide open.

"What sort of healthy, nourishing food?" Papa asked Mama as she sewed up his overalls.

"Vegetables right out of our garden, of course—and fruit from our orchard..."

"And what are we supposed to drink?" asked Papa.

"Try this," she said. "It's called water."

The next day the Bear family went to the supermarket to buy some sensible food for the pantry. Mama pushed right past the sweets and goodies and stocked up on whole-grain bread and cereal and fresh milk and cheese. Then she chose some fine-looking oranges and bananas—two fruits that didn't grow in her orchard.

CANDY
CHEESE
MILK

While she was waiting in the checkout line, someone said, "I'm glad to see that cartload of nutritious food, Mama Bear." It was Dr. Grizzly, the Bears' family doctor. "You must believe in good food for a healthy body."

"I certainly do," said Mama. "But I'm not sure about the rest of my family."

Dr. Grizzly took a look at Papa and the cubs.

"Hmm," she said. "I see what you mean. They look like they could use a little professional advice. Stop by my office tomorrow, please."

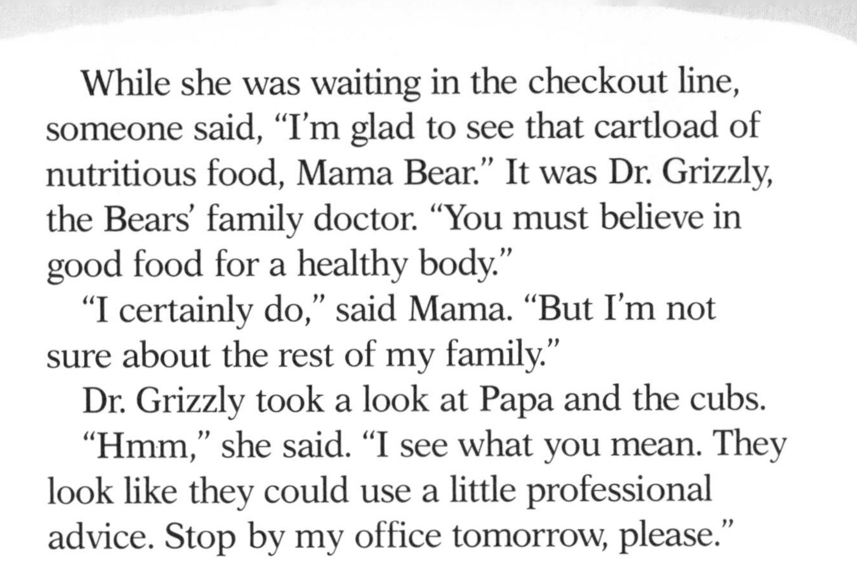

The cubs were nervous when they all arrived at the doctor's office the next day. "Do you think she'll give us some sort of shot?" they wanted to know.

"I don't think so," said Mama.

But with Dr. Grizzly, you never knew.

"Step in here, please," said Dr. Grizzly.

"Oh, boy! Movies!" said the cubs when they saw a projector and screen.

"Not exactly," said the doctor as she turned off the lights. "We're going to have a little slide show."

"About what?" asked the cubs.

"You'll see," she said, and started the show.

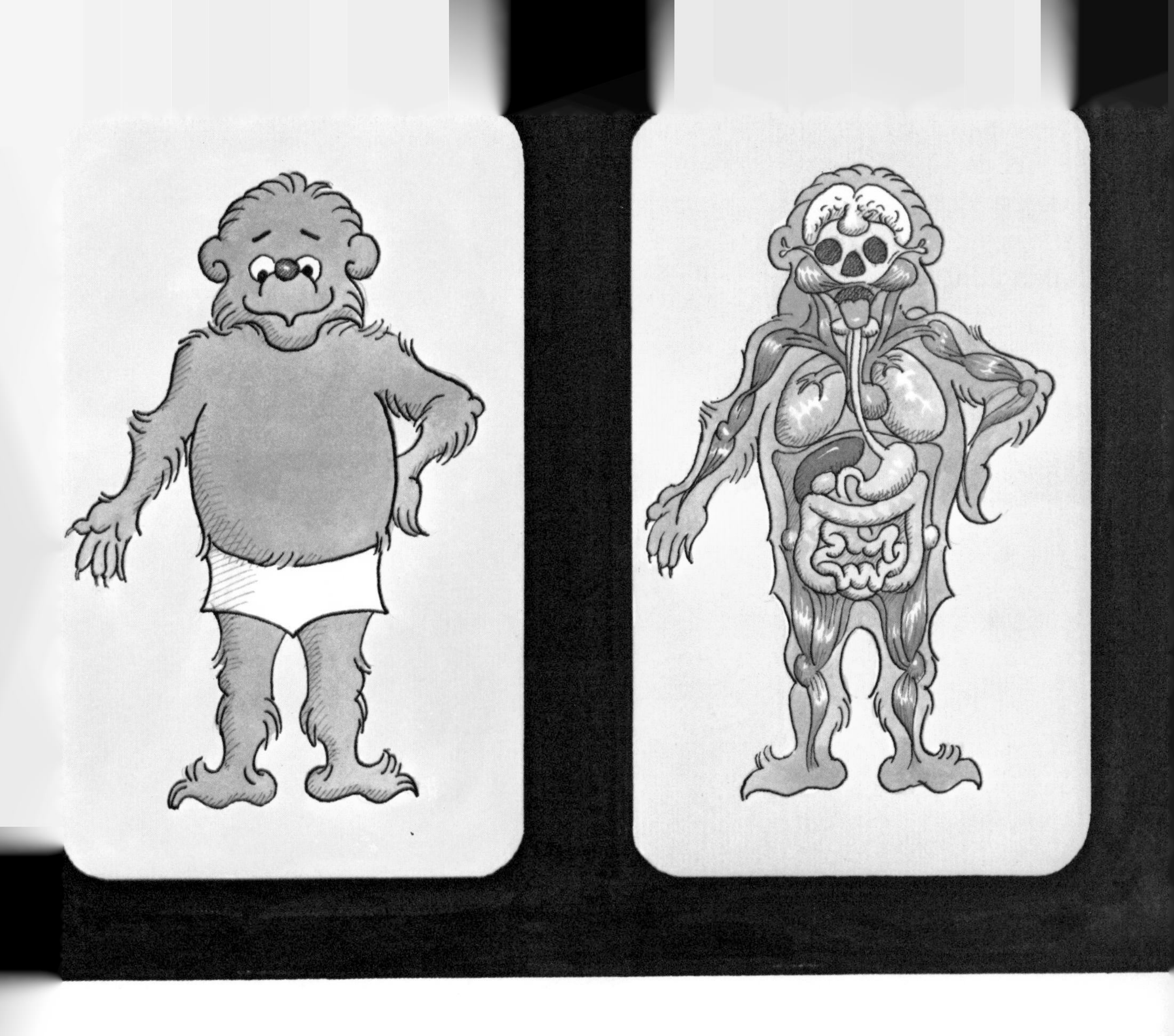

“This . . . is what your body looks like from the outside.

And this . . .” she said, changing the slide, “is what it looks like on the inside.”

“Wow!” said the cubs.

"Our bodies are a marvelous system of parts called *organs*, and it's these parts working together that let us do all the wonderful things we can do—climb mountains, sing songs, hit home runs, ride bikes. . . . It's a number of systems, really:

a system of nerves that lets us feel and think . . .

a system that keeps the blood flowing throughout the body. . .

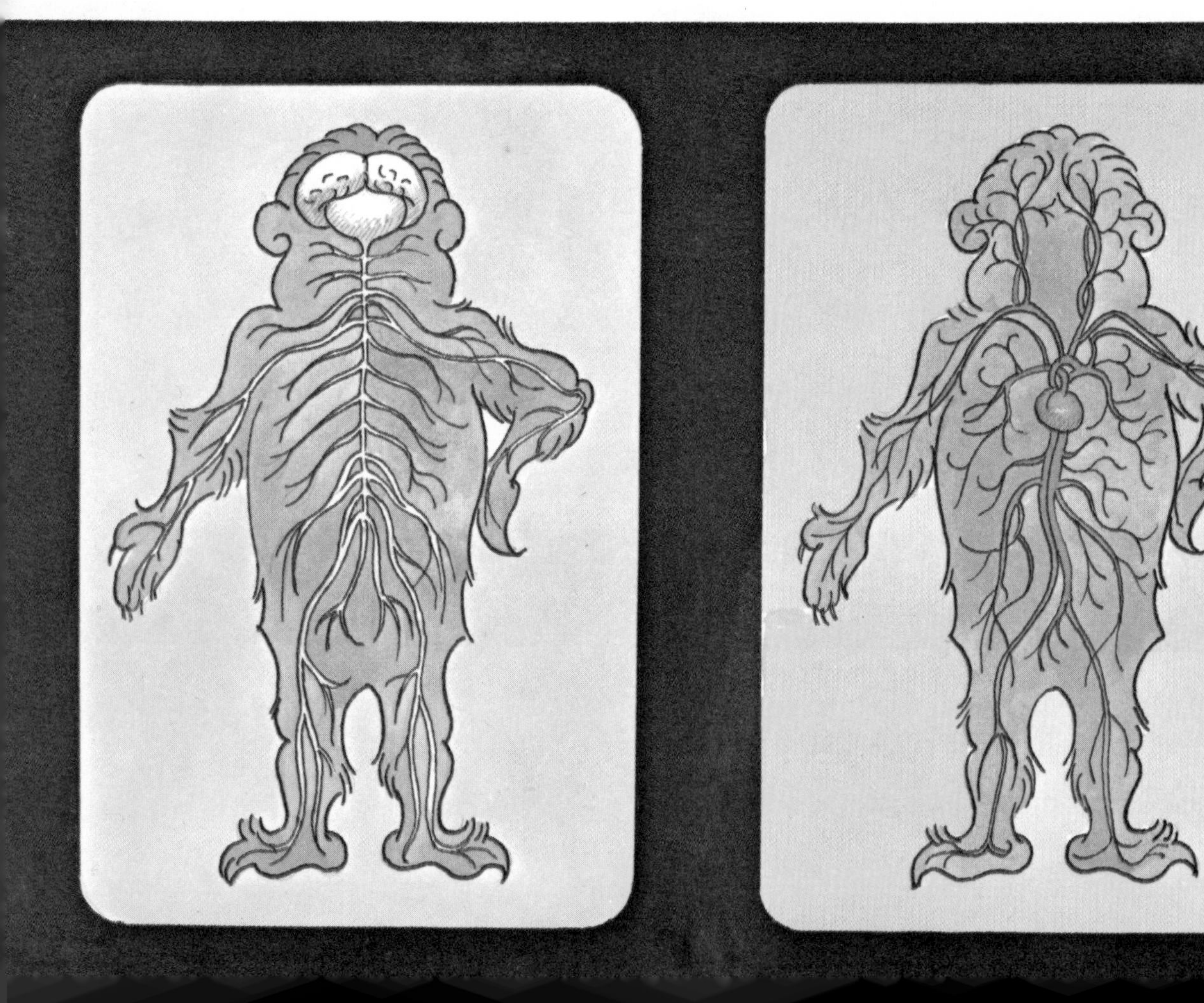

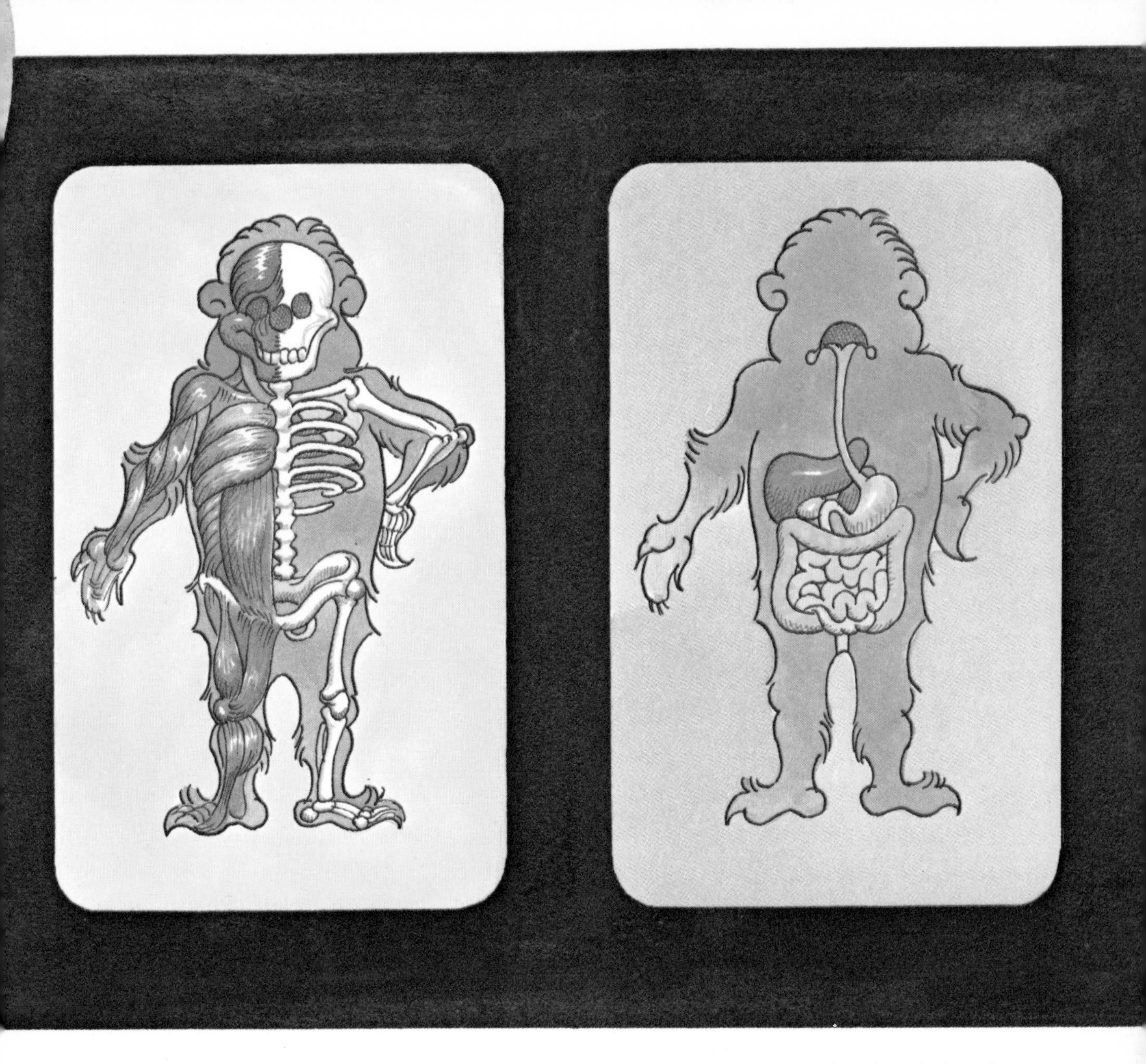

a system of muscles and bones that lets us move and gives us strength . . .

and a system for food that lets us take in the nourishment that gives us energy and keeps all the other systems healthy."

The last slide showed different kinds of foods and told how they helped the body. Papa looked for Sugar Balls and Choco-Chums, but they were nowhere to be seen.

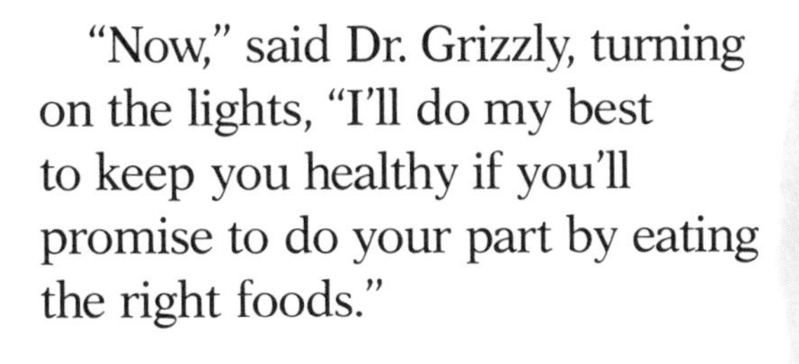

"Now," said Dr. Grizzly, turning on the lights, "I'll do my best to keep you healthy if you'll promise to do your part by eating the right foods."

"We promise!" said Brother. But Sister had a question. "About sweets and goodies—what *harm* do they do?"

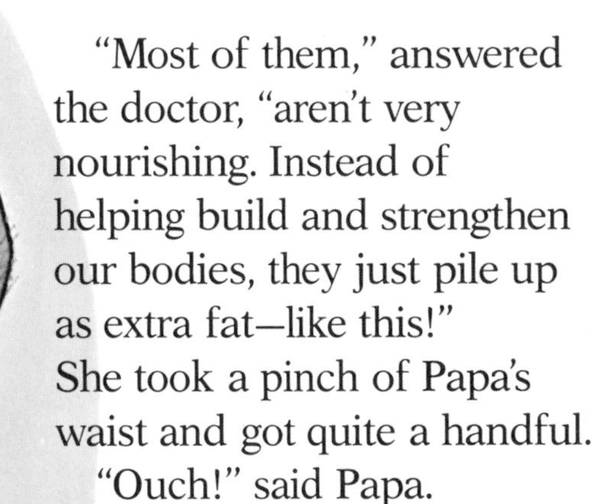

"Most of them," answered the doctor, "aren't very nourishing. Instead of helping build and strengthen our bodies, they just pile up as extra fat—like this!" She took a pinch of Papa's waist and got quite a handful.

"Ouch!" said Papa.

"And even worse—they fill you up, so you're not hungry for the food your body really needs."

And as the Bears were leaving–
"Just a minute!" she added.
"Uh-oh! A shot!" thought the cubs.
But that wasn't it at all.
"Exercise!" called the doctor. "An exercise program is important for good health too–and it will work off those extra inches!"

"Well," said Brother, "there's no time like right now—let's jog home!" And off went the cubs with Papa puffing behind.

At first it was a little strange eating just good, healthy food. For a while they could almost taste the Sugar Balls and Choco-Chums they weren't snacking on.

But Mama was always ready with *healthy* goodies . . .

apple slices for TV. . .

nuts and raisins for
the movies . . .

frozen yogurt at the mall . . .

and crisp, crunchy carrot
sticks just about anytime.

The Bears started a family program of jogging and exercise. So when the Bear Country Three-Mile Run was announced, they were all slimmed-down and ready.

Though they didn't win, they didn't come in last, either—not even Papa. And they won a prize for being the only family to finish the whole race. They were all excited and proud—especially Papa.

“I know what!” he said. “Let’s celebrate by opening up the freezer and–”

“Have a carrot stick!” interrupted Brother.

“And some nuts and raisins!” added Sister.

And Papa did.